For Jemima Appleton ~ **L A C**

For Amberin ~ **J D**

STRIPES PUBLISHING
An imprint of Little Tiger Press
1 The Coda Centre, 189 Munster Road,
London SW6 6AW

A paperback original
First published in Great Britain in 2014

Text copyright © Lucy Courtenay, 2014
Illustrations copyright © James Davies, 2014
Cover illustration copyright © Antony Evans, 2014

ISBN: 978-1-84715-439-2

A CIP catalogue record for this book is available
from the British Library.

Printed and bound in the UK.

10 9 8 7 6 5 4 3 2 1

MONSTER MOON!

L A COURTENAY

**ILLUSTRATED BY
JAMES DAVIES**

Stripes

MEET THE
SPACE
PENGUINS...

CAPTAIN:
Captain T. Krill
Emperor penguin
Height: 1.10m
Looks: yellow ear patches and noble bearing
Likes: swordfish minus the sword
Lab tests: showed leadership qualities in fish challenge
Guaranteed to: keep calm in a crisis

FIRST MATE (ONCE UPON A TIME):
Beaky Wader, now known as Dark Wader
Once Emperor penguin, now part-robot
Height: 1.22m
Looks: shiny black armour and evil laugh
Likes: prawn pizzas and ruling the universe
Lab tests: cheated at every challenge
Guaranteed to: cause trouble

PILOT (WITH NO SENSE OF DIRECTION):
Rocky Waddle
Rockhopper penguin
Height: 45cm
Looks: long yellow eyebrows
Likes: mackerel ice cream
Lab tests: fastest slider
in toboggan challenge
Guaranteed to: speed through
an asteroid belt while reading
charts upside down

SECURITY OFFICER AND HEAD CHEF:
Fuzz Allgrin
Little Blue penguin
Height: 33cm
Looks: small with fuzzy blue
feathers
Likes: fish fingers in cream and
truffle sauce
Lab tests: showed creativity
and aggression in ice-carving
challenge
Guaranteed to: defend ship,
crew and kitchen with his life

SHIP'S ENGINEER:
Splash Gordon
King penguin
Height: 95cm
Looks: orange ears and chest
markings
Likes: squid
Lab tests: solved ice-cube
challenge in under four
seconds
Guaranteed to: fix anything

LOADING...

CRRRUMP!

I am ICEcube, on-board guidance computer for a fish-shaped spacecraft named the *Tunafish*. My brain is very large, but my patience is very thin.

The Space Penguins have crashed into me twice this morning. Chief Engineer Splash Gordon's new invention – ride-on Penguin Manoeuvring Units, or PMUs – may be fun, but their brakes don't work. The ship's metalwork is dented. The floor is scratched.

My database says: Ow.

Ever since the Space Penguins made a

dramatic escape from the planet Splurdj and returned twelve small furry PomPoms to their home planet of Azimus Pi in the darkest, most remote corner of the universe, they have been fidgety. Back on Earth they happily did the same thing every day. Fish, toboggan, waddle, sleep. Out here in deep space they have discovered something new.

Boredom.

This is what they have been doing to kill time:

Captain Krill has a new exercise plan. He has waddled up and down the ship so many times that he has worn the floor completely smooth.

Our pilot Rocky Waddle has flown us straight through dangerous asteroid belts just for fun.

Chef and Security Officer Fuzz Allgrin has cooked star-whale blubber three hundred and sixty-four ways and clogged up the ventilation shafts with grease.

And Splash has built four PMUs with bad brakes. He is now test driving one of them on Captain Krill's newly smoothed floor. It's an accident waiting to happen.

CRRRUMP!

Recalibrating…

It's an accident that just happened. Captain Krill's exercises, Fuzz's new star-whale blubber dish, a tricky asteroid-belt move from Rocky and a PMU brake failure have all just come together in one big messy heap.

Excuse me while I short circuit.

ZZZPPPFFF.

CHAPTER ONE

STIR CRAZY

Captain Krill lay on his back with a large blob of star-whale blubber pie dripping from the end of his beak.

"What the curly cuttlefish just happened?" he asked, staring up at the metal rivets on the spaceship's ceiling.

Splash climbed off his crashed PMU and stared at the brakes with his flippers on his hips. "Darned if I know. I've adjusted the hydraulic pressure on this one at least ten times."

"OW-WOW-WOW!" Fuzz roared, hopping up and down while rubbing his feet with his flippers. "You ran over the Captain's belly, my feet *and* my star-whale blubber pie, Splash! You are so not getting a Christmas present this year."

"It must have happened while I was doing my exercises," said the Captain, raising his head to gaze at the track marks on his tummy.

"How are the sit-ups coming along, Captain?" Splash asked.

"I did one," said Captain Krill proudly.

"My fault, sorry," said Rocky from the flight deck. "A monster asteroid fragment was coming straight towards us. I had to take evasive action."

"No blubber pie for dinner, guys," said Fuzz, still hopping. "Unless you want to lick it off the Captain's face."

"Shame," said Rocky. "NOT."

"Say that again, barnacle brain," said Fuzz.

Rocky jumped out of his pilot's chair with his flippers raised and his eyebrows bristling. "With pleasure."

"No fighting on deck," said Captain Krill from the floor.

"We all need a change of scene," said Splash. He helped the Captain to his feet. "ICEcube? Find us a planet where we can stop and stretch our legs."

"Mine don't stretch very far," said Fuzz.

ICEcube's circuits whirred into life.

"Planet Flogiston. Little known, but sometimes visited by traders for its natural supply of metal, which grows in tree-like forms all over the planet. Surface temperature: seventy-five degrees Celsius, on account of the numerous volcanoes.

Journey time: three hours and fifteen minutes."

"Anywhere colder?" asked Rocky hopefully. "And maybe less volcanoey?"

"Planet Bitnipi. Surface temperature: minus two hundred and eighty degrees Celsius. Covered in mountainous permafrost."

"Perfect!" exclaimed the Captain.

"Journey time: thirty-two years, two hundred and two days," ICEcube continued.

The penguins groaned.

"It had better be Flogiston then," said the Captain.

"Flogiston is orbited by a small icy moon named Serac," ICEcube added. "Surface temperature: minus one hundred and three degrees Celsius. Journey time: two hours and forty minutes."

"Why didn't you mention that before?" said Splash.

"You asked for a planet," said ICEcube. "Not a moon."

"Duh," said Fuzz.

"Set the coordinates, Rocky," said Captain Krill.

Rocky whooped. "Serac, here we come!"

Far away, in section L of the universe, a little alien and a large robot were sneaking through the dark streets of the planet Kroesus's main spaceport. The little alien scuttled along, clattering its claws and swivelling its eyes. Clatter, clatter. Swivel, swivel.

"We need to get out of here," whispered Crabba. "I only gave that prison guard a tiny nip with my poisonous claws. He'll wake up soon, and then the whole of Kroesus will know you've escaped."

CLANK. CLANK. CLANK.

The robot behind Crabba was huge. Rusty. Cobwebbed. Unmistakably penguin-shaped.

"Boss?" said Crabba. "You look like you spent the last three months in a wet jail cell full of argon bugs."

Dark Wader's robot eyes glowed red. He flicked a glowing blue bug off his shoulder with a rusty flipper. "I did."

"I know," Crabba sniggered. "It was a joke."

"You think three months in a Kroesan jail cell with a lunatic pig-like cellmate is a joke?"

Crabba cringed. "Bad joke. Bad Crabba."

"The guards will barbecue Skyporker for not raising the alarm," said Dark Wader. He looked thoughtful.

"Should I have rescued him as well?" asked Crabba.

"No," said the pengbot. "Anadin Skyporker has been nothing but trouble since he tagged along with us after the Superchase Space Race. He would just slow us down. I want the Space Penguins, Crabba. Those putrid prawns will pay for what they did to me."

"I've arranged transport," said Crabba at once. "We'll be out of here in two clicks of my claws."

They emerged on to a busy street full of soldiers, traders and yellow-skinned Kroesans with lots of arms. Crabba scuttled towards a small ship docked in a bay.

"Here she is," he said proudly. "The *Sprout*."

Dark Wader looked at the craft. "It has no landing gear, Crabba."

Crabba looked dismayed. "It had landing gear when I left it."

"It has no windscreen, either. It has also lost its tailfin, both its wings and its thrusters."

Crabba stared at what was left of the *Sprout* sadly.

"Shouldn't have left it there, mate," said a rasping voice. "Thieves always nick stuff off ships docked there."

A purple, bull-like alien was leaning against a sleek golden ship docked beside the remains of the *Sprout*. He had a ring through his nose and a set of curly horns on his head.

"Who are you?" Dark Wader demanded.

"Balderdash Bigbutt. My friends call me... Well, they don't call me anything because I don't have any friends. But I do have a ship. She's called the *Lovely Loot*."

He patted the side of his golden spacecraft. Then he looked at Dark Wader's red eyes, his rust patches and his cobwebs.

"I know who *you* are, by the way," he said. "There's a reward for catching you."

"Already?" gasped Crabba. The eyes on his claws swivelled madly from side to side, looking for danger.

"The news is on every screen in town." Bigbutt pointed a massive thumb at an overhead screen. The words BREAK OUT and ROBOT PENGUIN and REWARD scrolled past in a bright, blinking ribbon of light. "Kroesans don't like it when their prisoners escape. I could make a fortune just by handing you over."

"I'll pay you more than the reward to get me out of here," said Dark Wader.

Bigbutt's sharp yellow teeth gleamed. "What are you offering?"

"More than you've ever had. And I'll double it if you track down four Space Penguins and help me get rid of them once and for all."

"Penguins?" said Bigbutt. "I eat penguins for breakfast."

Dark Wader smiled. "We will work well together. Come, Crabba."

Crabba kicked what was left of the *Sprout* before following his boss aboard the golden ship.

"Bigbutt?" he muttered. "Bighead, more like."

CHAPTER TWO

A FUNNY SORT OF TOOLBOX

Rocky brought the *Tunafish* down to land on the icy surface of Serac.

"Finally," said Fuzz.

"I thought ICEcube meant turn *right* at the shrimp-shaped nebula," said Rocky, as the penguins unbuckled their seatbelts. "OK?"

The Space Penguins wriggled into their spacesuits and boots, and waddled out into the chill and dark of the little moon. The ice glistened under their feet, and the distant stars twinkled high above their helmets.

"It's perfect," said Rocky happily.

Fuzz threw himself at a long, slidy stretch of ice just beside the *Tunafish*'s doors. He went so fast that the others lost sight of him almost immediately.

"I just went faster than a sailfish on skates," Fuzz said through his headset, sounding breathless. "You guys have to try it."

Rocky zoomed after Fuzz.

Captain Krill turned to Splash. "I might have a go myself," he said.

"I don't recommend it, Captain," said Splash, examining the ice under their feet. "The surface looks smooth, but it is embedded with thousands of razor-sharp ice crystals. It will rip your spacesuit to pieces."

There was a crackle on Captain Krill's headset.

"Small problem with our spacesuits,

Captain," said Rocky.

"The ice has ripped them to pieces?" said Captain Krill.

"How did you know?" said Rocky in surprise.

"Waddle back to the ship for repairs," Captain Krill ordered. "You must not damage your suits any further. They keep you alive out here."

The two penguins came waddling over the horizon, safe but rather tattered.

"Hmm," said Splash, examining the hundreds of tiny rips on the fronts of their suits. "I think I have a solution."

He lifted his belly to reveal the egg-shaped toolbox on his moon boots. Setting the box down on the ground, Splash opened it and took out a spray can.

"While I was making final adjustments to the brakes on the PMUs, I treated the runners with an extra-tough coating." Splash waved the spray can. "This is not only tough, but resistant to the most extreme temperatures. If I coat your damaged suits with it, it will hold the rips together."

"And then we'll be able to slide around this place completely unharmed?" said Fuzz hopefully.

"Exactly," said Splash. "I'll do it with my suit and the Captain's too. You never know when an extra-tough coating might come in useful."

"You really are a genius," said Rocky admiringly.

"It takes several hours to dry," Splash warned.

"Change into your spare suits and we'll play with the PMUs for a while," suggested Captain Krill.

The brakes on the PMUs worked much better outside than on board the *Tunafish*, mainly because there was more room to stop. The coating on the runners made them slide brilliantly. When they got tired of racing them over the ice, the Space Penguins discovered how to pilot the little vehicles by using the jet thrusters in the controller arms to lift off. Splash finished coating the damaged suits and joined in.

"I'm flying!" shouted Fuzz, zooming around above Captain Krill.

"I love these things," said Rocky, flying above Fuzz. "What do these buttons do?"

He jammed his flippers on the two black buttons set at the facing ends of his vehicle's controller arms.

With no warning, Fuzz's PMU shot upwards and clanged into the base of Rocky's, where it got stuck. Fuzz was knocked out of his seat at the impact.

"I'm not flying any more!" cried Fuzz, as he plummeted to the ground.

The two PMUs were stuck firmly together. Rocky pressed some more buttons, but it was no good. Rocky and both vehicles landed upside down on the ice in a crumpled heap beside Fuzz.

"Rocky, you tuna brain," said Splash angrily. "You activated the electromagnets. You've wrecked both vehicles!"

"So much for your extra-tough coating," sniggered Rocky, climbing out from underneath his broken PMU.

"Fight!" shouted Fuzz.

Captain Krill waddled between Rocky and Splash. "I'm sure Rocky is very sorry about wrecking the PMUs," he said.

"He doesn't look it," Splash complained. He loaded the PMUs back on to the *Tunafish* and stomped on board.

Captain Krill noticed that Splash had left his toolbox lying on the ground. It was rocking gently from side to side.

I wonder what's in there? the Captain thought. His Ship's Engineer was in no mood for questions, so he decided not to ask. Instead he picked it up, tucked it under one flipper and followed the others aboard.

"I have a new star-whale blubber dish
to try on you at dinner," said Fuzz, trying to
lighten the atmosphere. He took off his spare
spacesuit and hung it up. "It's quite chewy,
but the flavour isn't as bad as normal."

"Whoopee," Splash grumbled.

"There's no need to be snarky with
Fuzz," Rocky said. "His food mostly tastes
of octopus bum, but he does his best."

"Cheers, Rocky," said Fuzz. "I think."

"You left this outside, Splash," said the
Captain, putting

Splash's egg-shaped
toolbox down on
the side.

Splash
picked it up
and waddled
wordlessly
to the engine
room.

"My flippered friend needs to chill," said Rocky. "Speaking of which, I'm going to hang out in the freezing-fog room before dinner. Anyone want to join me?"

They ate dinner in silence. Partly because Splash wouldn't talk to anyone, and partly because the star-whale blubber was too chewy for conversation.

As soon as dinner was over, Splash disappeared back into the engine room. Fuzz cleared the table while Captain Krill practised another sit-up. Rocky took his seat at the controls and started plotting a new course through the stars.

"ICEcube," he said, "were you serious when you said that Bitnipi place was the nearest penguin-friendly planet?"

"I do not tell jokes," said ICEcube. "But my data for this part of the universe is inaccurate. Much of it is uncharted."

Captain Krill finished his sit-up and gazed out of the window at the volcanic red planet of Flogiston, not far beyond Serac.

"According to ICEcube, metal traders occasionally pass this way," he said. "Put out a call, Rocky, see if you can find a friendly alien to talk to. Nothing beats local advice."

Rocky put out a message on the intergalactic web.

"Advice needed on cold planets in the area. Contact the *Tunafish*."

A screen by Rocky's head flickered into action almost immediately. A four-eyed pilot grinned at the penguins, showing a mouth full of gold teeth.

"This is the *Clanger*, calling the *Tunafish*," he said. 'How much will you pay for this information?"

"Tell him to go away," Captain Krill said crossly. "We'll find someone more polite."

Rocky tapped a few buttons and leaned into the screen. "*Clanger*, this is the *Tunafish*," he said. "We won't pay you a pilchard. We don't deal with rude rust buckets. Yours sincerely, the Space Penguins."

The alien stopped grinning his golden grin. "Suit yourselves," he snarled. The screen went blank again.

"Set the coordinates for Bitnipi," Captain Krill said at last. "The longest journey must start with the smallest waddle."

Rocky did as he was told. The *Tunafish* lifted away from the surface of Serac and zoomed into the darkness. Large and red, Flogiston faded behind them like a dying bonfire.

Back in the engine room, Splash put his goggles on top of his head and studied his toolbox curiously.

When the Captain had given it to him outside the ship, it had felt warm in his flippers. As Splash examined it more closely, he realized two things. Firstly, he couldn't open it any more because it appeared to have lost its catch. Secondly, it *wasn't* his toolbox.

It was an egg.

Splash put the egg on his feet and tucked his tummy over the top. His own father had done it to him, when he was an egg, so it felt like the right thing to do. The egg was heavier than his toolbox, and Splash found it difficult to waddle around. It was his turn to be a father now. But a father of what?

CHAPTER THREE

CUDDLES

Balderdash Bigbutt's ship, the *Lovely Loot*, was fast and well equipped. Dark Wader clanged up and down, admiring the golden fittings, the rows of weapons that hung on the walls and the larder full of delicious food.

"Where did you get all these pulse pistols?" he asked Bigbutt.

"Stole them," Bigbutt said.

"What about that bazooka blammer?"

"Stole it."

"And all the caviar in the kitchen cupboards?"

"Bought it in a caviar sale," said Bigbutt. "Ha, ha, GOT YOU. Stole it."

"I luuuurve your horns," said Crabba. "Did you steal them too?"

"Ripped them off the last owner's head," Bigbutt grunted. "I quite fancy a pair of poisonous claws next."

Crabba went quiet and started polishing the rusty bits on his boss's helmet.

The intercom crackled.

"Message for the *Lovely Loot*. This is the Kroesan Space Port Authority. You have left port without the necessary authority. We suspect that you are carrying an escaped prisoner. Return to port or we will activate our mechanical meteor defence system against you."

"I'd like to see you try, dumbos," Bigbutt sneered down the intercom.

"What are you doing, Bigbutt?" said Dark Wader in alarm, as a flaming meteor came blasting towards the *Lovely Loot*. "The Kroesan mechanical meteors are extremely dangerous and—"

Bigbutt pressed a button. There was a flash and the strange feeling of being squished down to nothing. Then suddenly, where they had been looking at a flaming meteor, there was nothing but deep dark space before them. Dark Wader blinked.

"Where did the meteor go?" Crabba squeaked.

"About ten thousand light years away," smirked Bigbutt.

"You have a hyperspace drive?" said Dark Wader, relaxing. "Impressive. Where did you get it?"

"Stole it. Tell me about these penguin mates of yours," said Bigbutt.

The pengbot's eyes flashed red again. "They are not mates."

"They were once, boss," Crabba piped up.

"Shut up and polish, Crabba," snarled Dark Wader. "The Space Penguins are the boil on my bottom, Bigbutt. The wasp in my helmet. The gristle in my grub. Find them and you will be richly rewarded."

Bigbutt posted a message on the intergalactic web.

"This is the *Lovely Loot* calling.

Any word out there on the location of four Space Penguins and their ship the *Punyfish*?"

"It's *Tunafish*," said Crabba, sniggering. "This guy's an idiot, boss. Let me—"

A four-eyed alien pinged on to the screen, looking annoyed.

"*Lovely Loot*, this is the *Clanger*. Four penguins called me a rust bucket over the spacewaves a few hours ago. I would normally charge for information, but I am offended and will give you their most recent location for free."

"That was easy," said Crabba sourly. "I could have done that with one claw."

"Ha!" Dark Wader laughed gleefully, as Bigbutt noted down the coordinates. "Time for your hyperspace drive again, Bigbutt. Wouldn't you agree?"

"We need more fuel before we can activate it again," said Bigbutt. "There's a nasty asteroid belt we have to cross to reach the fuelling station, but we'll be fine." He patted the *Lovely Loot*'s control panel. "I can fly this baby like a rocket."

"It *is* a rocket," said Crabba.

"Shut up and let Bigbutt do his job, Crabba," said Dark Wader. He clanged his flippers together. "Let's go!"

"I'm worried about Splash," said Captain Krill, as Rocky piloted past a hurtling meteor. "We haven't seen him for three days now. It's very unlike him to sulk for so long."

"I even apologized through the engine-room door," said Rocky.

"I've been leaving out food for him," said Fuzz. "He's been eating it, so he must be OK."

Rocky and Fuzz watched as the

Captain waddled towards the engine-room doors, lifted a flipper and knocked.

"Who's there?"

"This is your Captain speaking," said Captain Krill.

The engine room door opened just a crack. Splash peered out. "Yes?"

The Captain smiled brightly. "Is … everything OK?"

"Fine." Splash shut the door again.

Captain Krill waddled back to the flight deck and sat down at the table. "Something's not right," he said.

"He's probably just working on a new invention," said Fuzz.

"When he's inventing we hear banging and explosions," said the Captain. "We haven't heard anything for days."

"I am getting an unusual reading on our oxygen levels," ICEcube reported. "We appear to be using more than usual."

Captain Krill smoothed his ear patches. It helped him to think. Then he waddled back to the engine room and knocked again.

"What now?" asked Splash irritably, as he opened the door again.

The Captain thought he saw something behind his Ship's Engineer. He craned his neck to get a better look. Splash pushed him back and quickly closed the gap in the door so that only his beak poked through.

"What is it, Captain?" he repeated, a little more politely.

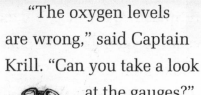

"The oxygen levels are wrong," said Captain Krill. "Can you take a look at the gauges?"

"Yes." The Captain squeezed one webbed toe into the closing door.

"Splash," he said, "is something in there with you?"

Splash went red. "No."

"Right," said Captain Krill, feeling relieved.

It was good to know he had been imagining things. The creature he thought he'd seen had been rather odd. Small and grey, with a big bubble on its head.

"I'm just ... working on my toolbox,"

said Splash. "Now if you'll excuse me, I have an oxygen gauge to check and a new toolbox catch to fit."

Captain Krill removed his toe. The door clanged shut.

"There's nothing to worry about," he told the others, as he waddled back to the flight deck. "He's working on his toolbox."

"That toolbox?" said Rocky.

He pointed at the egg-shaped toolbox sitting on the floor beside the engine-room door.

The egg had hatched two days earlier.

"Who's a coochy little Cuddles then?" Splash said fondly to the very uncuddly creature sitting by his feet.

Cuddles was iron grey in colour, and had grown so much in the last two days that he was already half as big as Splash.

He had spines on his back and a tough, leathery coat. He had a whip-like tail, six scaly legs and one enormous tooth on the end of his nose. But the oddest thing about Cuddles was the transparent orb that covered his entire head like a space helmet.

In two days, the long tooth on the end of Cuddles's nose had grown faster than anything else. The spiky tip was almost touching the orb now. Splash wondered what would happen when it did.

There was a third knock on the door. Splash sighed and went to answer it. "The oxygen gauges are fine, Captain," he began.

Captain Krill lifted up the toolbox so that Splash could see it.

There was a long pause.

"Thank you," said Splash, taking the toolbox. "I wondered where that was."

"Weren't you working on it?" Captain Krill asked.

Behind Splash, the tip of Cuddles's nose tooth made a funny squeaking noise as it rubbed against the head orb.

"Of course not!" Splash said quickly. "I'm working on my *other* toolbox."

He slammed the door just in time.

POP.

The creature's nose tooth pierced the orb, which fizzled away into nothing.

"Arf!" said Cuddles in a croaky little

voice. He started sniffing at a box of bolts lying on the floor, opened his mouth and sucked in the whole lot like a scaly grey vacuum cleaner.

"You eat metal!" said Splash, delighted. "Hold on a minute…"

He hunted around in his cupboards, and gave another box of bolts to Cuddles. The creature vacuumed it up at once. Splash gave him a third box of bolts, a box of nails and a very small box of screws. Cuddles sucked up everything.

"Arf!" he said after each mouthful. "Arf! Arf!"

But Cuddles still seemed to be hungry.
And when he started hoovering up one of
the copper cables connecting the generator
to the ship's lighting system, Splash
realized he had a problem.

"Do you think we should all charge in?"
asked Captain Krill. "There's definitely
something in there with Splash."

"You think we have an intruder on
board?" Rocky said anxiously.

"I'm up for charging in, if you are," said
Fuzz, flexing his flippers. "I'm totally up
for charging in, even if you're not."

"I would advise caution," said Captain
Krill.

"Caution is for codfish," said Fuzz.
"NINJA PENGUIN!"

He rushed towards the engine-room
doors.

Then suddenly the lights went out.

CHAPTER FOUR

YUM YUM

There was a skidding noise and a clang in the darkness.

"OW!" Fuzz roared.

"I told you to be cautious," said Captain Krill. He couldn't see his own flippers. Outer space was always dark, but this was crazy.

There was a whirring sound from the back-up generator. Temporary lights flicked on along the *Tunafish*'s walls, casting a strange yellow glow.

"I'm getting reports that Dark Wader has escaped from the planet Kroesus," said ICEcube suddenly. "He was last seen jetting in this direction in a ship called the *Lovely Loot*."

"That's all we need," said Captain Krill grimly.

"But he's supposed to stay in jail for at least a hundred years!" said Rocky in shock. "He is so going to kick our penguin butts for putting him there."

"He'll never find us," said Captain Krill, sounding more confident than he felt. "We're light years from anywhere civilized."

Fuzz sat up, rubbing his head where he'd banged it on the wall. "But if he does," he said in a menacing voice, "we'll be ready."

Splash burst out of the engine room. "Nothing to worry about," he said wildly.

He waved his toolbox around. "I'm fixing the lights now."

"I demand to know what's going on, Splash," said Captain Krill.

Fuzz picked himself up off the floor and rubbed his beak. The main lights buzzed and came back on.

"See?" Splash said, breathing hard. "All. Under. Control."

"Right," Captain Krill said slowly.

Splash slammed the engine-room door.

The Captain headed towards the freezing-fog room. Too many strange things were happening, and it was making his brain ache. He needed to chill out.

The room wasn't quite as cold as usual. The Captain flicked a switch and waited for lovely cold fog to come billowing out of the vents.

Splat. Splat. Splat-splat-splat.

Gobbets of star-whale blubber grease started oozing through the vents instead. Captain Krill backed out and decided to try the ice-bath room. H e opened the door. Clouds of scalding steam poured towards him from the boiling bathtub.

"SPLASH!" the Captain bellowed, waddling away from the steam and the grease. "I'M COMING INTO THAT ENGINE ROOM WHETHER YOU LIKE IT OR NOT!"

He climbed up the ladder to the main deck, puffing and blowing.

"Everything all right, Captain?" asked Splash, leaning casually against the engine-room door.

Captain Krill smoothed his ear patches. "Grease in the freezing-fog room. Steam in the ice-bath room. *What are you hiding in there?*"

He pushed his Ship's Engineer aside.

If anything, the engine room looked emptier than usual. None of Splash's usual boxes of spare nuts and bolts were lying around. The workbench had no tools on show. The room had been swept clean of the usual metal shavings that littered the floor. Several copper cables looked as if they had been hastily mended and looped high up on the ceiling.

Fuzz followed Captain Krill into the room and looked around.

"Almost as tidy as my kitchen in here, Splash," he said.

"According to the control panel, there's been a power surge in the extra-cold store," Rocky shouted from the flight deck.

Splash hurriedly stood on the trapdoor leading from the engine room to the extra-cold store. "Don't go in the extra-cold store," he said.

"Why not?" Fuzz asked.

"I tried chaining him up, but he ate the chain," said Splash.

"WHO IS IN THE EXTRA-COLD STORE?" demanded the Captain in his most captainly voice.

Splash's shoulders slumped. "Cuddles," he said.

The extra-cold store was a mess. Star-whale blubber lay on the floor, minus its cans. Tinless sardine pâté was smeared on the walls. Wing-pong balls rolled from side to side, minus their metal boxes.

Cuddles looked up from sucking the metal bottoms off Splash's magnetic-soled moon boots. His whip-like tail lashed, sending blobs of sardine pâté flying. "Arf!" he said in a friendly sort of way.

"He started off as an egg!" Splash said helplessly. "You gave him to me instead of my toolbox, Captain."

Captain Krill stared at Cuddles.

"But what is he?"

"Arf!" said Cuddles. "Arf! Arf!"

"Species: Flogisaur," said ICEcube helpfully. "Flogisaurs thrive on the planet Flogiston, feeding on the constant supply of metal. During breeding season, Flogisaurs fly up to Flogiston's moon, Serac, and lay their eggs."

"Awesome," said Rocky.

"Flogisaurs have pressurized scales designed for space flight," ICEcube continued. "The new hatchlings fly down from Serac to join their parents on Flogiston before their head orbs burst."

"What head orb?" said Rocky, looking at Cuddles.

Splash wriggled. "It already burst."

"He's ugly, isn't he?" said Fuzz.

Splash bristled. "He's not. He's beautiful."

The others looked dubiously at Cuddles, who had abandoned Splash's moon boots to suck the metal handles off a pile of wing-pong bats.

"What are we going to do with him?" asked Rocky.

"Keep him?" Splash said hopefully.

"Arf!" said Cuddles. He made a puking noise and spat out a pile of bolts on the extra-cold store floor. He hoovered them up again almost at once.

"We can't keep him," said Captain Krill. "Look at this mess. We have to turn the *Tunafish* around and return him safely to his parents on Flogiston."

Cuddles burped. He opened his mouth and started hoovering the metal bolts out of the floor itself.

"No way, stingray," said Fuzz. "Now he's eating the ship!"

All the Space Penguins, even Splash, looked at the little Flogisaur in horror. They were light years from anywhere. How long did they have before there was no *Tunafish* left?

CHAPTER FIVE

COUNTDOWN

The Space Penguins huddled around
ICEcube. In the background, Cuddles
was sucking Splash's welding torch. He
finished it and burped.

"It's clear what we have to do," said
Captain Krill. "Give Cuddles a sedative to
send him to sleep. One for all and all for…"

"FISH!" said Fuzz and Rocky.

"He won't like that," said Splash
unhappily.

"It's him or the ship," the Captain

pointed out. "We'll keep him where we can see him. Everyone follow me."

"Arf!" cried Cuddles.

Splash scooped him up with difficulty – he was getting bigger all the time – and carried him back up the ladder to the flight deck after the others.

Rocky turned the *Tunafish* round and set it to full cruising speed while the others tried to get the little Flogisaur to sleep. It was harder than they expected. Cuddles drank a whole bottle of SleePeeZee with no effect, slurping up the metal cap for afters. He swallowed a box of Snooz-FX, spat out KipperWile and gargled SnorSumMor before spitting the lot at Splash and eating the metal legs off the dining table, which hit the floor with a clang.

"Now what?" said Splash, wiping Snooz-FX pills, KipperWile and SnorSumMor off his feathers.

"Fly like there's a leopard seal on our tails," said Captain Krill grimly.

"Or a robot penguin," Fuzz added.

The Captain, Fuzz and Splash waddled off to different corners of the ship to find enough metal to feed Cuddles for the journey. What could the spacecraft spare?

Wires, old piping, rusty tools. Rivets from the walls and ceiling. The ice-bath taps, rungs from the ladders that led from the bottom deck of the *Tunafish* to the top. The legs from the wing-pong table and the dining chairs, Rocky's eyebrow comb, Splash's second and third best toolbelts. And…

"NOT MY SAUCEPANS," Fuzz warned, barring the way to the kitchen.

"It's the only way, Fuzz," said Captain Krill.

"It's not Cuddles's fault he's so hungry," said Splash, as Cuddles munched through a coil of steel rope. "He's growing!"

"Arf!" Cuddles agreed.

Fuzz had to stand aside. Even the PMUs had to go. The penguins piled everything they had in front of the Flogisaur – and crossed their flippers.

Meanwhile, the *Lovely Loot* was zooming at record speed through an asteroid belt in section M of the universe.

"Do you have to go so fast, Bigbutt?" squealed Crabba, watching through his claws as Bigbutt narrowly missed an asteroid the size of Antarctica.

"Your boss wants to catch penguins,"
Bigbutt growled, speeding up even more.
"We need fuel to catch penguins. We're
nearly at the fuelling station."

The *Lovely Loot* shuddered as a jagged
asteroid scraped over its roof.

"They'll be light years away by the time
we reach those coordinates!" said Crabba
in a trembling voice.

Bigbutt patted a shiny golden box
set into the control panel. "Top-of-the-
range space nav," he said. "Guaranteed to

locate other spaceships within a hundred thousand light years of their last known whereabouts."

"Don't tell me," said Crabba, rolling the eyes on the tips of his claws. "You stole it."

"Course I stole it," Bigbutt boasted. "I steal everything."

"We will catch them," said Dark Wader. "And when we do, guess what?"

Guess the End of the Space Penguins was Dark Wader's favourite game.

"You'll fire them out of the *Lovely Loot*'s space cannon," suggested Crabba weakly, as another asteroid flew by with millimetres to spare.

"I'll build a special spiky basketball hoop," giggled the big pengbot. "And score a hundred baskets each with those flightless freaks."

"You'll pump them into penguin

balloons and pop them with your beak," Crabba groaned.

"What did these penguins do to you?" said Bigbutt with interest.

"They hatched before I could turn them into omelettes," said Dark Wader in a dark and terrible voice. "How much further, Bigbutt?"

"I'm in charge of the star charts," Crabba moaned. "Not the cowhead."

"Better a cowhead than a crusty little creep," growled Bigbutt, accelerating towards a cluster of asteroids that were too close together for comfort. "Not far now. In twenty minutes, we'll be fuelled up and hitting that hyperspace button before you can say … I dunno, something long and complicated."

"Like 'brain'," muttered Crabba.

CHAPTER SIX

"OH, GUPPY GUTS..."

Cuddles ate through every lock and door the Space Penguins put in his way. After three days of flying back towards Flogiston with a hungry, fast-growing Flogisaur aboard, there wasn't much left of the *Tunafish*.

"Any sign of our destination, Rocky?" asked Captain Krill tensely.

Rocky's pilot chair had disappeared down Cuddles's throat two days earlier. Now Rocky was barely tall enough to see through the *Tunafish*'s windscreen. "There's a red thing coming up," Rocky said, as Splash hoisted him up so he could see out a little better. "So that's hopeful."

There was every chance that the red thing wasn't Flogiston at all, given Rocky's terrible sense of direction. The penguins tried not to think about that.

Splash suddenly dropped Rocky and looked around what was left of the flight deck. "Where's Cuddles?"

Rocky got back on to his feet, rubbing his head. "I haven't seen him."

"If he's found my last saucepan, I'll put him into a casserole," Fuzz threatened.

"If he's found your last saucepan, you won't be able to make a casserole," Captain Krill pointed out. "Keep flying, Rocky. As you know, Cuddles ate the auto-pilot mechanism yesterday, so we need you at the helm at all times. The rest of you, follow me. We need to find that Flogisaur."

Captain Krill, Splash and Fuzz tracked Cuddles to Splash's engine room and the ventilation system. The grilles had gone. So had most of the metal tubing that filtered the air around the spaceship.

"Arf!" said Cuddles, in an echoey sort of way, deep inside the vents.

Splash wrung his flippers. "I think Cuddles has eaten through the ventilation system and found the hull."

"That's the outside of the ship," said Fuzz. "Right?"

Splash nodded.

"If Cuddles finds the hull, will he eat it?" checked Captain Krill.

Splash wrung his flippers again. "Yes. And then the hull will stop protecting us and the cabin will stop being pressurized and we'll all be sucked into the vacuum of outer space."

"In other words, we'll all go pop?" Rocky shouted from the flight deck.

"Exactly," Splash said.

"I will tempt Cuddles back inside the ship with my last saucepan," Fuzz said heroically.

He fetched the saucepan and dangled it in front of the gaping

ventilation hole. There was a loud sucking noise deep inside the vent. In the snapping of a clamshell, the saucepan was pulled from Fuzz's grasp. The little penguin gaped at his empty flipper.

"You slurping squid-for-nothing!"
he shouted furiously. "You iron-eating
imbecile! You … metal-munching maniac!"

"Arf!" came Cuddles's echoing answer.

"I'll have to go out there to strip the
landing gear of its metal plating and
reinforce any breaches in the hull," said
Splash.

"Right," said Captain Krill. "What?"

"I'm going on a spacewalk to stick the
outside of the ship back together again,"
Splash explained.

"Definitely Flogiston coming up, guys,"
Rocky called down the passageway.

Splash slid down the rungless ladder to
the extra-cold store to fetch his spacesuit.
"I would advise everyone to put their
spacesuits on," he said. "In case we lose
pressure before we reach Flogiston."

The Captain and Fuzz joined Splash
in the extra-cold store, where they put on

their extra-toughened suits. Fuzz helped Splash put on his moon boots.

"Good luck out there," Fuzz said, as Splash headed for the airlock. "Remember to hold on."

Splash patted his boots. "The magnets on the soles will hold me in place. And I plan to tether myself to the ship with a hundred metres of knitting wool, left over from a Christmas jumper I've made for the Captain. I'd prefer the usual steel rope, but Cuddles ate it. Tell Rocky to keep flying whatever happens."

With quite a lot of puffing, Captain Krill struggled back up the ladder to take Rocky's spacesuit to him at the controls.

"Not long until we land, Captain," said Rocky, getting dressed as quickly as he could. "Hold on to your beak."

"An unidentified ship has just leaped through hyperspace ahead of us," said ICEcube. The computer's voice sounded a little distant because Cuddles had eaten most of its wiring.

Captain Krill was the only one who could see out of the windscreen. A sleek golden ship was speeding towards them like a bullet. He knew in a flash that the ship was the *Lovely Loot*.

Beaky Wader had found them.

Instinctively the Captain checked the state of the *Tunafish*'s weapons. Then he remembered that all the ship's pulse pistols, zap-o-blasters, bazooka blammers, stun guns, rocket launchers and space cannons were inside Cuddles's tummy.

"Well, *hello!*" said Dark Wader's voice down the intercom. He sounded extremely cheerful. "Fancy meeting you out here."

Captain Krill groaned. Of all the sections in the universe, Beaky Wader had to be in theirs. It just wasn't *fair*.

"Hello, Beaky," he sighed. "How did you escape from prison?"

"I'm called *Dark* these days, Krill, and you know it. And I escaped from prison because I'm brilliant. Do you like my new ship? She has a hyperdrive, you know. The *Tunafish* is looking very scrappy. What have you done to her?"

The Captain wasn't about to tell his arch-enemy how much metal they'd stripped from the *Tunafish* to feed Cuddles. Not now Flogiston was so close.

"It's called 'streamlining'," he lied. "She goes a lot faster now."

"She looks like she's about to fall apart," Dark Wader sneered. "Mind you, she always looked like that."

"Is that *Beaky* I can hear?" said Fuzz with excitement, waddling on to the flight deck. "I've missed him. Hey, mackerel-breath!" he shouted down the intercom. "Fancy a fight?"

"I'll prime the guns, Wader," said a rough

voice the Space Penguins didn't recognize.

"Thank you, Bigbutt," said Dark Wader.

Rocky burst out laughing. "Seriously, Beaky? You've found a friend called *Bigbutt*?"

"What's so funny?" said Dark Wader crossly.

"Bigbutt…" gasped Fuzz, leaning against the wall with one flipper and hooting.

"What do you want, Beaky?" Captain Krill had to raise his voice over Fuzz and Rocky's shrieks of laughter.

"Your total extermination, of course," said the pengbot. "Bigbutt? Fire!"

On the other side of the ship, Splash was emerging from the external hatch. He tied one end of the wool to his toolbelt and the other end to the door hatch.

He checked his tools one more time.

Then he stepped out on to the hull,
settling his moon boots firmly on the metal
fuselage so the magnets on the soles would
hold him in place.

The *Tunafish* lurched sideways and a
space cannonball exploded over his head.
With horror, Splash realized they had
company.

Then he realized something a whole lot
more important.

Cuddles had sucked the magnetic soles
off his boots.

"Oh, guppy guts," he gulped.

And he started floating
away from the
Tunafish into the
vast darkness
of space.

CHAPTER SEVEN

NO ESCAPE

Captain Krill picked himself up off the floor as the *Tunafish* spun upright again. "Too close for comfort, Rocky," he panted. "That space cannonball missed us by a catfish whisker."

"Sorry…" Rocky struggled to control what was left of the *Tunafish*'s flight instruments. "I … I was laughing so much that … that I hit the wrong button…"

"Bigbutt!" Fuzz howled, lying on the floor and clutching his belly.

Captain Krill suddenly saw Splash drift past the windscreen of the *Tunafish*. He was still holding on to the length of wool attaching him to the ship – but only just.

"Galloping goujons!" he gasped, clapping a flipper to his forehead.

Following the Captain's gaze, Rocky and Fuzz stopped laughing and goggled in horror at their friend.

"Help!" shouted Splash, though no one could hear him. "I'm sorry I never did the washing up when I said I would, Fuzz! I'm sorry I drove that PMU over your belly, Captain! I'm sorry I put superglue in your eyebrows, Rocky! HELP!"

Two things happened at once. The *Lovely Loot* dived – and Splash landed face-first on its windscreen.

"Oh goody-goody goldfish," said Dark Wader down the intercom. "We have a penguin hostage. Bring him in, Crabba!"

The Space Penguins could only watch as a hatch in the *Lovely Loot*'s belly popped open. A metal claw snaked out to catch Splash round the waist and haul him inside. Then a steel rope shot out of

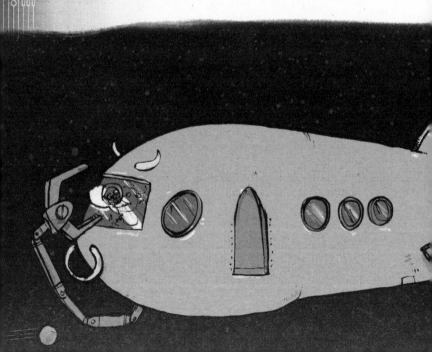

the *Lovely Loot*'s tail, looped round the
Tunafish and went taut.

"So," said Dark Wader in a chatty sort
of voice. "I have your Ship's Engineer.
I have your ship. What will happen next,
I wonder? Surrender or I'll throw Splash
back out into space. You have ten minutes."

The intercom clicked off. The Space
Penguins stared at each other.

"What are we going to do?" groaned
Rocky.

"Splash will give that flightless maniac a waddle for his money," said Fuzz. He shook a flipper out of the windscreen at the *Lovely Loot*. "Short-circuit his wires, mate! Fuse his brain!"

There was a sudden noise behind them. Cuddles had come out of the vents and was peering through the kitchen door with a greedy look in his eyes. He was so big now that he could hardly fit through it.

"Leave my kitchen ALONE!" roared Fuzz.

He waddled at top speed towards Cuddles. The Flogisaur blinked uncertainly, and shot back into the vents again with its scaly tail tucked between its six legs.

"You scared him, Fuzz," said the
Captain sternly.

They could all hear a whimpering
"Arf!" from deep inside the ship. Cuddles
sounded like he wouldn't be coming out
for a while.

"Now perhaps he'll stay out of trouble,"
said Fuzz. "Focus, team! It's time to fight
that pongy pengbot and rescue Splash!"

"Rocky," said Captain Krill suddenly.
"Can you fly us directly underneath the
Lovely Loot?"

"Easy as eel pie," said Rocky. "What's
the plan?"

Captain Krill clasped his flippers
behind his back. "A steel rope links our
two ships. We're already in our spacesuits.
If we hide underneath the Lovely Loot,
Wader won't be able to see us as we climb
the rope and board the ship by surprise."

"What about weapons?" said Rocky.

"We haven't got any!"

"We'll have to use our wits instead,"
said the Captain.

"It's the most dangerous plan you've ever
suggested, Captain," said Fuzz. "I love it!"

Rocky brought the *Tunafish* gently
underneath the *Lovely Loot*. Within
moments, the penguins were scaling
the rope leading up to the belly of Dark
Wader's new ship.

"What do we do when we get there,
Captain?" Fuzz asked through his headset.

"We sneak aboard and free Splash,"
Captain Krill answered. "Then we fly
down to Flogiston, release Cuddles, repair
the *Tunafish* and leave again."

"You make it sound so easy, Captain,"
Rocky said.

The Space Penguins went silently up the
steel rope, flipper over flipper, their booted
feet floating behind them. Soon they were

clustered around the *Lovely Loot*'s external hatch. Captain Krill gently turned the handle and the penguin astronauts slipped inside. Easing open the connecting airlock, they entered a long room where a tall pengbot was standing, alone and unarmed.

Dark Wader swung round. "Krill!" he gasped.

Captain Krill took off his helmet. "Yes, it's me," he said.

"Me too," said Rocky.

"Me three, whale wee," said Fuzz.

"Where's Splash?" Rocky demanded.

"I don't know," said Dark Wader with a shrug of his metal flippers.

Captain Krill noticed the way the pengbot's red eyes had flicked towards a small door set in the wall.

"Aha!" He strode towards the little door. "You can't fool the Space Penguins, Beaky. Splash is in there, isn't he?"

"I don't know what you're talking about, Krill," Dark Wader smirked.

Captain Krill rattled the handle. "It's locked," he told the others.

"Try the key," suggested Fuzz. He pointed to the key in the lock.

"I was going to," said Captain Krill with dignity.

He took the key with both flippers and turned. At once, he glimpsed Splash sitting tied up inside a small golden room.

"It's a trap!" shouted Splash, struggling

against his ropes. "Waddle for your life, Captain!"

Crabba and a big bull-like alien the Captain had never seen before leaped out of nowhere and shoved him hard from behind. He tumbled into the room beside Splash.

"Get them all, Bigbutt!" Crabba crowed.

"Fight, team!" shouted Captain Krill, as Rocky and Fuzz roared with laughter.

"Can't," Fuzz gasped, chopping weakly at Bigbutt.

"Laughing … too much…" Rocky moaned, kicking aimlessly at Crabba's claws.

SLAM! The door was locked behind the struggling penguins. Dark Wader, Bigbutt and Crabba grinned at them through a little window.

"I thought you said these penguins were clever, Wader," sneered the bull-like alien.

"My mistake," said the pengbot. "Welcome aboard, old friends. Make yourselves comfortable. Bigbutt, Crabba and I plan to land on Flogiston shortly, where we will help ourselves to all the lovely free metal that grows there. You, meanwhile, will land a bit earlier than that."

Bigbutt sniggered.

"What are you planning, Wader?" Captain Krill demanded.

"It was Bigbutt's idea," said Dark

Wader. His red eyes gleamed. "But I think it's terrific. You know that Flogiston is covered in volcanoes?"

"Yeeees," said the Captain. He didn't like where this was going.

"We're going to drop you in one on our way to land," said Crabba gleefully.

"You'll sizzle like sausages when you hit the lava," said Dark Wader. "Doesn't that sound marvellous?"

The penguins looked at their feet. The floor of their golden prison was one massive trapdoor.

"There really is no escape," said Wader.

"Landing in ten minutes, Wader," growled Bigbutt, checking the large gold watch on his hairy purple wrist. "Losing the penguins in five."

"Eat my flippers, Hugebum," said Fuzz.

"No thanks," smirked Bigbutt. "I don't like fried food."

"Oh, ha ha, Giant Buttocks, you think you're so clever," Rocky shouted.

But Dark Wader, Bigbutt and Crabba had already disappeared.

"Now what?" said Fuzz.

Captain Krill untied Splash. "We prepare to die as nobly as narwhals," he said.

"No way, stingray," said Splash. He ran his flippers thoughtfully over his toughened spacesuit. "Put your helmets back on, guys. We're in for the ride of our lives."

The *Lovely Loot* rocketed through the hot
smoky atmosphere of Flogiston. The planet's
famous volcanoes came into view, spouting
red-hot magma, throwing glowing rocks
into the air and blasting out clouds of thick
black ash. Sitting at the *Lovely Loot*'s control
panel, Bigbutt expertly dodged the dangers.

Dark Wader pointed through the
windscreen at a mega-massive fiery
mountain ahead, whose steep sides ran
with boiling lava.

"Let's drop the penguins in that
one!" he said, clanging his metal flippers
together with excitement.

"Yes, yes, yes!" crowed Crabba, and
clattered his claws.

Bigbutt gave a nasty smile. And as the
Lovely Loot flattened out near the top of
the volcano, he pressed a button to open
the trapdoor and send the penguins to
their fiery doom.

CHAPTER EIGHT

ALL TOGETHER NOW

The four Space Penguins felt the trapdoor opening beneath their boots.

"Hold on to the bars until I say go!" Splash shouted through his headset.

"Can I just say that I don't like this plan much?" Rocky shouted back.

The penguins grabbed on to the golden bars of their prison as the floor disappeared. Despite their protective spacesuits, they could feel the heat from the bubbling cauldron of lava below. They

dangled there like Christmas decorations
for several long hot seconds until the far
side of the crater came into view.

"GO!" ordered Splash.

The space mates obeyed. They
brought their flippers into their sides and
sped through the clouds of smoke like
bullets.

"I hope this works, Splash," Captain
Krill shouted.

"So do I," Splash shouted back.

BOOOM! The volcano erupted beneath
them, throwing up a fountain of fire and
rock.

"THIS WASN'T IN THE PLAN!" roared
Rocky, flapping his flippers in fright. "We
were just going to slide down the side of
the crater, not land in the middle of a fresh
eruption!"

They landed on top of the spewing
flames, toppled on to their bellies and

started shooting down the mountainside on a great red wave. Splash's extreme-temperature coating on their spacesuits was working.

"This ... is ... awesome," Fuzz gasped through his headset. His helmet was fogging up with the heat.

"I am on FIRE," Rocky roared. He did a somersault over a lumpy bit of lava and landed perfectly back on his belly. "I am SMOKING!"

The bottom of the volcano rushed towards them. With one final WHOOSH, they bumped down a slope of black pebbles and landed on the charred ground with a bounce.

"Talk to me, Rocky," Captain Krill said urgently, staggering to his feet. "Are you alive?"

"Never been better," panted Rocky.

"You said you were on fire!"

"I was the hottest penguin in the universe." Rocky got to his feet and dusted off the black, sooty belly of his spacesuit. "But not literally."

"Again!" Fuzz shouted, clapping his suited flippers.

"Look who's over there, guys," said Splash.

The *Lovely Loot* had landed a hundred metres further on, in the heart of a forest of glittering metal trees. Still attached by the *Lovely Loot*'s steel rope, the *Tunafish* lay beside it. Dark Wader, Crabba and Bigbutt were tearing metal off the trees, uprooting it from the ground and loading it on to the golden ship. They hadn't noticed the penguins.

"Let's clobber them," said Fuzz enthusiastically.

"And get in the way of *those* guys?" said Rocky in a faint voice.

The Space Penguins boggled at the sight of two enormous iron-grey creatures galloping towards the *Lovely Loot*, their massive tails lashing behind them and their vast hoover mouths open wide.

"Fully grown Flogisaurs," said Splash in awe.

Dark Wader's metal beak clanged open in shock. He whacked Bigbutt and Crabba to get their attention. "Run!"

The Flogisaurs were almost on the *Lovely Loot* when they suddenly swerved sideways and hoovered a perfect hole in the side of the *Tunafish*.

"Our SHIP!" Rocky yelled in horror. "Get off, you great greedy groupers!"

But as they watched, Cuddles zoomed out of the hole in the side of the *Tunafish*. The creatures brought their thin tails together in a great twisting knot of delight.

Cuddles had found his family.

In the mad scramble to get away from
the Flogisaurs, Dark Wader seemed to
buckle. He staggered, lost his balance and
landed on his back.

"Beaky could use some of your
heatproof coating, Splash," said the
Captain. "Flogiston is too hot for his
runners."

"What are we waiting for, guys?" Fuzz
demanded. "Let's nick the *Lovely Loot* and
tow the *Tunafish* out of here!"

"Arf!" Cuddles cried. He sucked a long
metal branch off one of the trees and spat
it in the penguins' direction. It landed by
Splash's feet with a clang.

"Did you see that?" Splash said to
the others, picking up the stick of metal.
"Cuddles gave me a present. Bye, Cuddles!
Be good for your other daddy!"

The penguins sneaked aboard the
golden ship, the metal branch still

clasped in Splash's flippers. Through the windscreen they could see Dark Wader ordering Bigbutt and Crabba to help him up.

Captain Krill pulled off his helmet and smoothed his ear patches. "We shouldn't steal this ship," he said. "It's against space regulations."

"Hugebum dropped us in a volcano," Fuzz said indignantly. "I think we deserve his ship."

Splash looked at the piles of metal branches that Bigbutt, Beaky and Crabba had already loaded on to the *Lovely Loot*. "There's enough metal here to mend the *Tunafish* and replace everything Cuddles ate," he said. "We can tow the *Tunafish* to Serac, make our repairs there and leave the *Lovely Loot* behind when we're finished. That's not stealing. It's borrowing."

"When we've mended the *Tunafish*, we could do more ice sliding in our toughened suits," said Rocky happily. "And Splash can rebuild the PMUs. After all this excitement, boring little Serac feels like the perfect place for a holiday."

Captain Krill nodded. "Borrowing, not stealing. I can live with that. Fire up the thrusters, Rocky."

Rocky pressed a button on the control panel. The *Lovely Loot* thrummed smoothly beneath the penguins' feet.

"I love the sound of a well tuned engine," said Splash.

"Nice saucepans," said Fuzz approvingly, as he checked out Bigbutt's kitchen cupboards.

The steel rope tightened on the *Tunafish* as the *Lovely Loot* lifted off the scorching ground, towing the fish-shaped craft behind it. Already Cuddles and his family looked tiny. Beaky, Bigbutt and Crabba were even smaller.

Two tears rolled off Splash's beak as he waved through the windscreen. "Bye, Cuddles," he shouted.

"Bye, Beaky," said Captain Krill more cheerfully.

"By the way, Beaky's going to be seriously annoyed with us now," said Rocky.

"He wasn't before?" Splash asked.

The *Lovely Loot* blasted through Flogiston's atmosphere, setting its nose towards Serac.

Fuzz emerged from a kitchen cupboard and waved a big jar of caviar at his space mates.

"Anyone for a snack?" he said.

P.S.

"POO POOPY POO-POO-POO!" Dark
Wader shrieked. "How are we going to get
off this boiling nightmare of a planet now?
My runners are melting!"

Quickly, Crabba pointed a claw at
Bigbutt. "It's all his fault, boss."

Bigbutt gawped at the empty Flogiston
sky and burst into tears.

"My SHIP!" he bawled, like a toddler
with a burst balloon. He stomped his feet.
"THEY ST ... ST ... STOLE MY SHIP!"

"You stole it first," Crabba sniped.

"BUT IT WAS LOVELY AND GOLDEN
AND M ... M ... MINE!" wailed Bigbutt.

"Oh, grow up, Butthead," said Crabba.
"We have bigger problems right now."

The adult Flogisaurs had started
grazing on the large metal trees nearby.
But the smaller one was padding towards
them, his eyes fixed on Dark Wader's

shiny metal-plated body.

"WAAAH!" Bigbutt weeped.

"What was that thing doing on board the *Tunafish* in the first place?" said Dark Wader irritably. "And what is it looking at now?"

"You," said Crabba.

And the scaly little alien sat on his claws to hide his eyes as the creature opened its odd-shaped mouth and slurped.

HAVE YOU COLLECTED THESE OTHER SPACE PENGUINS ADVENTURES?

STAR ATTACK!

Emergency! When a stricken spacecraft
sends out a distress call, the penguins
dive to the rescue beak-first – straight
into the jaws of a mysterious space
station and some rather fishy business.
Will they escape? Or will the intergalactic
heroes be stuck there forever?

COSMIC CRASH!

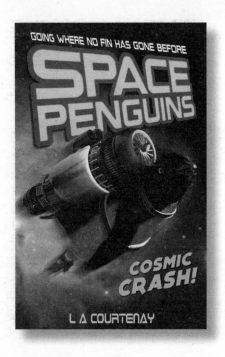

Alert! Alert! When the penguins
splash-land on a watery planet, they
find themselves in the tentacles of a
monstrous sea creature. Can they escape
with their ship in one piece or are they
well and truly sunk?

GALAXY RACE!

Zoom! Pilot Rocky is desperate to enter the
Tunafish into the Superchase Space Race.
But this is the most dangerous race in
the universe. And when an old enemy
turns up at the start, the penguins find
themselves up to their beaks in trouble!

METEOR MADNESS!

Action stations! The Space Penguins are attacked by a fleet of starships and escape by the skin of their flippers. But as they head on their way, Captain Krill notices his crew are acting strangely. It looks like there's double trouble ahead in the shape of some rather shifty impostors...

PLANET PERIL!

Prepare for landing! When the penguins arrive on slimy Planet Splurdj, they're impressed by the entertainment the Oozis have on offer – especially the new Space Zoo. But will the penguins find out what the slippery Oozis are really up to before it's too late?

Lucy Courtenay has officially been
writing children's fiction since 1999,
and unofficially for a lot longer than that.
She has contributed to a number of series
for Stripes including ANIMAL ANTICS
and, most recently, SPACE PENGUINS.
In her spare time she sings with the
BBC Symphony Chorus and forages for
mushrooms, which her husband wisely
refuses to touch. If she were a penguin,
she would be a rockhopper. Her eyebrows
are already fairly awesome.